Brad's Birthday Cake

Story by Dawn McMillan   Illustrations by Pat Reynolds

"Look, Grandma," said Ella.

"I can see Brad outside his house."

"Hello, Brad," she called.

Grandma said hello to Brad, too.

Brad came over to the fence.

"Hello, Mrs Scott. Hello, Ella," he said.

"It's my birthday on Sunday. I'm going to be seven. Will you come to my birthday party, Ella?"

"Yes, please," said Ella.

On Saturday morning,

Ella said to Grandma,

"I want to make a present for Brad.

Can we make him

a surprise birthday cake?"

"Yes," said Grandma.

"Let's make the cake now."

The next day, Grandma said,
"I will get the birthday candles."

"But we can't put candles
on Brad's cake," said Ella.
"He won't see them."

"You are right," said Grandma.

"There are some big peppermints in this bag!" said Ella.

"Let's put them on Brad's cake. He can't see candles, but he can smell peppermints."

"Clever girl!" said Grandma.

Grandma iced Brad's cake
and Ella put seven peppermints
on top.

Ella took the cake
to Brad's house.

13

"Happy birthday, Brad," said Ella.
"Grandma and I made you
a surprise birthday cake."

"Thank you!" said Brad.
"I can smell peppermints
on my cake!"

"Yes," said Ella. "And I made a '7', with seven big peppermints!"